Life Skills

Ethics

**Doing the
Right Thing**

by Robert Wandberg, PhD

Consultants:
Roberta Brack Kaufman, EdD
Dean, College of Education
Concordia University
St. Paul, Minnesota

Millie Shepich, MPH, CHES
Health Educator and District Health Coordinator
Waubonsie Valley High School
Aurora, Illinois

LifeMatters
an imprint of Capstone Press
Mankato, Minnesota

Thank you to Heather Thomson of BRAVO Middle School, Bloomington, Minnesota; to Christine Ramsay of Kennedy High School, Bloomington, Minnesota; and especially to all of their students, who developed the self-assessments and provided many real stories.

LifeMatters Books are published by Capstone Press
PO Box 669 • 151 Good Counsel Drive • Mankato, Minnesota 56002
http://www.capstone-press.com

Printed in the United States of America

Library of Congress Cataloging-in-Publication Data
Wandberg, Robert.
      Ethics: doing the right thing / by Robert Wandberg.
          p.   cm. — (Life skills)
      Includes bibliographical references and index.
      ISBN 0-7368-0699-7 (hardcover) — ISBN 0-7368-8840-3 (softcover)
      1. Ethics—Juvenile literature. 2. Teenagers—Conduct of life. [1. Ethics. 2. Conduct of life.] I.
Title. II. Series.
      BJ1661 .W32 2000
      170—dc21   00-032263
                                                                     CIP

      Summary: Describes ethics and why teens should care. Discusses how to develop a code of ethics, how friends, family, and others can influence ethics, and how ethics affect the community. Includes self-assessments and hypothetical ethical situations.

Staff Credits
Charles Pederson, editor; Adam Lazar, designer; Katy Kudela, photo researcher

Photo Credits
Cover: UPmagazine/©Tim Yoon
©DigitalVision, 9
FPG International/©Michael Krasowitz, 7; ©Mike Smith, 27; ©Mark Scott, 39
Index Stock Imagery, 47
International Stock/©Scott Barrow, 13, 33; ©Patric Ramsey, 45
Photo Network/©Jeffry W. Myers, 17; ©Eric Berndt, 53
Uniphoto Picture Agency/©Bob Daemmrich, 19, 37; ©Mark Loader, 28; ©Llewellyn, 34; ©Joe Bailey, 57
UPmagazine/©Tim Yoon, 5, 15, 23, 31, 41, 51

Table of Contents

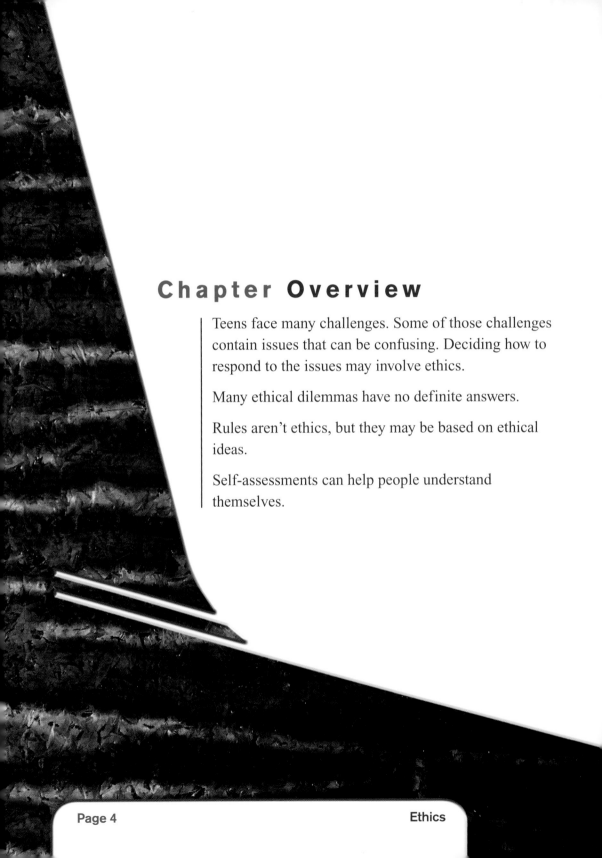

Chapter Overview

Teens face many challenges. Some of those challenges contain issues that can be confusing. Deciding how to respond to the issues may involve ethics.

Many ethical dilemmas have no definite answers.

Rules aren't ethics, but they may be based on ethical ideas.

Self-assessments can help people understand themselves.

CHAPTER 1

⌗

Ethics: What Are They?

Defining Ethics

An ethic is a standard of proper, moral behavior, or behavior that follows a standard of right and wrong. Ethical behavior is based on doing what you believe is right or acting in a manner that most people accept. Sometimes you have options that may not have definite answers. The choices and decisions in life can prompt a simple discussion of a topic or a heated debate.

Ethics aren't just something to think or argue about. They're practical, action-oriented ideas. Some experts have said that the practice of ethics has two parts. The first part is deciding what's right and wrong. The second part is to act on that decision and do the right thing.

One research study found that most first-year college students tend to believe every question has a "right" answer. By the time they have completed college, most students have discovered that there is no one answer to many moral questions. Students learn to make a choice and discover the "best" answer for them. They also realize they can understand and act on a decision and be responsible for it.

People's ethics can help them stay out of trouble. Teens may have trouble with parents, school staff, friends, or even the police because of ethical dilemmas, or problems. Some political leaders, sports heroes, or other celebrities have had trouble for not recognizing their behavior as unethical. Some problems don't have satisfactory solutions or may require a choice that does the least harm. In this chapter, **ComplexMatters** involves a range of ethics.

What's an Ethical Dilemma?

An ethical dilemma is a problem that may have no clear right or wrong answers. It requires a choice. Even doing nothing can be a choice. Most of the time, an ethical dilemma affects people besides you.

As a teen, you have more freedom and opportunity to make choices than you did when you were younger. You will face difficult situations that may require you to examine your beliefs. What you "knew" to be true may be different in new circumstances. For example, although you may have learned that you shouldn't drink, it may seem like all your friends drink. So, how do you know what to do? Your ethics can help you out.

Denzel and Heidi, Age 17

Denzel sees a man at the store drop a $20 bill on the floor. The man walks away without noticing.

Heidi's younger sister has started to hang around with a group of students who smoke and drink. They're all 14 years old.

Denzel and Heidi have several choices. Denzel could pick up the money and keep it, return it, or give it away. He could even leave it alone. Heidi could talk to her sister and her sister's friends. She might tell an adult or do nothing. Do Denzel and Heidi have ethical dilemmas?

"Ethics is a code of values which guide our choices and actions and determine the purpose and course of our lives."
—Ayn Rand, novelist and philosopher

In reading about Heidi and Denzel, you might have felt confused about what they should do. It would be helpful to know if the problem is an ethical dilemma. One way to decide is to answer these three questions. If you answer yes to any of them, it's an ethical problem.

1. Is there a behavior or choice in this situation that most people would accept?

2. Is there a specific behavior or choice that you believe is right?

3. Is there a specific behavior or choice that you believe is wrong?

Food for Thought

Here's some food for ethical thought. People can have all kinds of opinions about these situations. Is it ethical:

To have an abortion? to perform one? An abortion is the ending of a pregnancy.

For a woman to become pregnant and deliver a child in return for money?

Not to tell a person that he or she is dying?

To have laws against prostitution? This is having sex with someone in return for money.

To transplant animal organs into humans? to raise animals solely to use their organs this way?

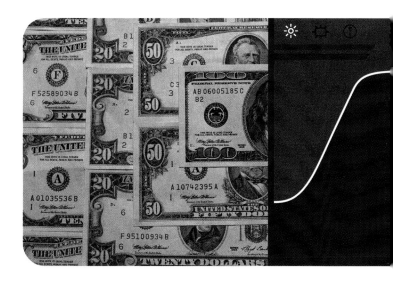

To spend large amounts of money on dying patients? to withhold treatment from dying patients?

For doctors to help people kill themselves?

For a professional to break rules of confidentiality? Should those rules be different for priests, doctors, or lawyers?

For dying people to use experimental drugs?

For gay and lesbian people to marry? These are men and women who are attracted to people of their own gender.

To give needles or drugs to drug addicts?

To treat patients who develop AIDS because of risky behavior?

To treat patients who develop lung cancer because of risky behavior?

To allow tobacco companies to sell cigarettes?

To surgically make it impossible for people to have children, even if they want children?

To base the quality of health care on how much money a patient has?

For students to play contact sports if they have HIV, the virus that causes AIDS?

Rules

Rules aren't ethics, though they normally exist to help people know what to expect from each other. They often are created to protect the safety and well-being of most people. Rules guide a person's, group's, or society's beliefs about what's normal and acceptable.

Schools have rules. For example, violence, destruction of school property, or possession of weapons are against the rules. Imagine that a student sells drugs at school. The student might be expelled, or the school might even have the student arrested.

Families often have rules. For example, teens are often asked to call home if they're going to be late. Like most rules, family rules often are meant to keep family members safe.

Sometimes, however, rules may seem unfair. For example, slavery was legal in the United States before the Civil War. Some religious groups believed slavery was wrong. Their ethics drove them to help runaway slaves. Most people agree that laws allowing slavery are bad. Some people's ethics may cause them to break such rules or laws.

Merriam Webster's Collegiate Dictionary traces the use of the word *ethic* in English back to the 1300s.

Self-Assessments and Ethics

Self-assessments are tests that can help us know ourselves better. There are many kinds of self-assessments. Some ask questions about knowledge, attitudes, or behavior. Some self-assessments might look at a person's risk for lung disease, alcoholism, or depression. Other topics might include ethical issues such as the death penalty or legalizing marijuana.

By assessing yourself from time to time, you can see how you change. The key to self-assessments is that only *you* interpret the information. Teens developed the following self-assessment, which shows what they believe is important regarding ethics.

How Ethical Am I?

Read items 1–14 below. Choose a number after each item that describes you best. Write it on a sheet of paper. Use this scale:

1 = Rarely   2 = Sometimes   3 = Most of the time

1. My behavior is acceptable.	**1**	**2**	**3**
2. I contribute to my personal health.	**1**	**2**	**3**
3. I contribute to the health of my family.	**1**	**2**	**3**
4. I contribute to the health of my friends.	**1**	**2**	**3**
5. I contribute to the health of my community.	**1**	**2**	**3**
6. I treat people fairly.	**1**	**2**	**3**
7. I face rather than ignore ethical dilemmas.	**1**	**2**	**3**
8. I can resolve ethical dilemmas.	**1**	**2**	**3**
9. I set moral guidelines for myself.	**1**	**2**	**3**
10. I follow my moral guidelines.	**1**	**2**	**3**
11. I respect the feelings of others.	**1**	**2**	**3**
12. I believe that the feelings of others matter.	**1**	**2**	**3**
13. I am responsible.	**1**	**2**	**3**
14. I know or can find out the right thing to do.	**1**	**2**	**3**

Add up your points. The closer your total is to 42, the more ethical behavior you probably practice. If you scored 1 or 2 on any items, think of ways you can improve in those areas.

Points to Consider: ComplexMatters

Do you think ethics are important? Why or why not?

What would you do in Denzel's or Heidi's situation? Why?

Choose one of the situations from the "Food for Thought" section on pages 8–9. Give your opinion and explain why you think that way.

Do you think the rules in your family are more strict than in families of other people your age? Why or why not?

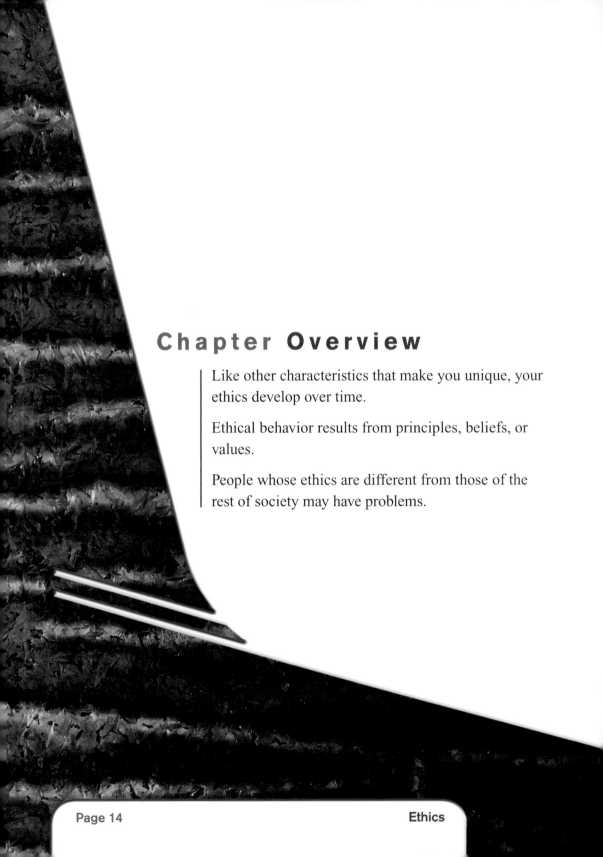

Chapter Overview

Like other characteristics that make you unique, your ethics develop over time.

Ethical behavior results from principles, beliefs, or values.

People whose ethics are different from those of the rest of society may have problems.

CHAPTER 2

Under Construction

You aren't like anyone else. You have unique fingerprints. No bar code determines your worth, and no factory can produce another person just like you. Your ethics are uniquely yours, too. In **EthicalMatters,** you will examine behaviors or events that cause conflicts inside you and with others.

Who Are You?

How you handle day-to-day events in your life helps build who you are. You may struggle, for example, with whether to skip school or tell a lie. You may hear an inner voice—your conscience—that may help provide your answer. The boundaries of right and wrong behavior for you are your ethics. Boundaries are limits you set on your behavior so you feel comfortable.

"There is no pillow so soft as a clear conscience."
—French saying

You have physical characteristics. You may be tall or short, straight or curly haired, dark or light skinned, male or female. You have talents. You might be musical, athletic, smart, a good listener, or artistic. Your personality may be outgoing, shy, dramatic, or reserved.

From the day you are born, you're under construction and your personality develops. You dream, set goals, and make decisions. Sometimes you celebrate. Sometimes you feel afraid, sad, and lonely. Your personality is uniquely yours.

You might have family and friends who also influence your ethics. Perhaps your family is large, with both parents as well as brothers and sisters at home. Maybe it is a smaller family with just you and a mom or dad. There might be stepparents or a guardian, grandparents, aunts, or uncles in your home. Your family may or may not be close and able to share feelings and ideas easily. These experiences are part of what makes your personality.

A Guide to Behavior

Ethics point you in a direction. If you were in a forest, which way would you hike to get out? There may be many paths, and you may not know what the next step will bring. In some ways, ethics are like a compass. An ethics compass may give you direction along the way.

Ethics form as you grow. As a child, you might follow some simple commands: "Play nicely. Share your toys." As you practice, the responses become automatic. For example, you might have an escape route designated to get out of the house if there's a fire. Everyone knows it and has practiced it.

Similar practice helps to avoid unhealthy situations. You can practice ethical behavior, too, such as positive health behaviors and making wise choices. For example, you can practice with a friend to refuse an offer of alcohol.

Ethical Behavior

An action based on a principle, belief, or value is sometimes called ethical behavior. It's a commitment to something you believe in strongly. It also involves doing the right thing.

Many societies throughout the world seem to strive for a certain set of ethics. These universal ethics include responsibility, trustworthiness, respect, fairness, caring, and citizenship. These ideas lead to specific behaviors. For example, trustworthiness may lead to such behaviors as being honest or being loyal to friends. Respect may lead to using good manners or not insulting others.

Ethics don't always provide concrete or clear choices. Sometimes the answers are easy and you know instinctively what to do. For example, you know you shouldn't break a car window to take someone's purse. Other times you may struggle when confronted with questionable behavior. This may be especially true when your friends or family are involved. For example, if your friend asked, should you let her cheat using your test answers? Your value of honesty may conflict with your value of loyalty to friends. You may have to decide which value is more important to you.

Not everyone may agree with a specific behavior. Ethical behavior is based on practices that can be defended, are logical, and that others understand. This means that people have reasons for what they do.

However, without an ethical standard, it would be impossible to judge whether people's personal values are right or wrong. The universal ethics mentioned before make it possible to judge whether a behavior is right or wrong. Without that set of ethics, judging between the behavior of Adolf Hitler and Mohandas Gandhi would be impossible. Both believed deeply in their ideas and thought they were the best ideas for everyone. Hitler's behavior led to the deaths of millions of people. Gandhi's ideas led nonviolently to India gaining its independence from Great Britain.

Lacy, Age 14

"I live in a small farming town where everybody knows everyone. On the first day of seventh grade, I met a girl who moved into town during the summer. Her name is Sherry, and she's African American. Her family is the first African American family ever to live in our town. Not all my friends are comfortable that I hang out with Sherry, so they just avoid us. In fact, one day one of my friends comes up and tells me that I can either be friends with her or with Sherry."

"I think a lot of the problems in my school occur because of the history of this country. Like right now, a lot of people think immigration is bad. But we're all based on immigration. My family came as immigrants and so did a lot of other people or their families. That's what makes this country what it is. There's a lot of ignorance, and people don't realize that everyone's going through the same thing."—Hashim, age 17

Ethical Dilemmas

As you learned in Chapter 1, an ethical dilemma may have no clear right and wrong answer. The answer may be, "It depends." Sometimes you do what you have to do, even if it means feeling alone. Some people face harm because of their beliefs and actions in ethical dilemmas. These people may be abused, insulted, injured, put in prison, or even killed. However, they may have believed that their short-term pain would gain long-term good for others.

Ethics and ethical behavior are important to everyone. For example, one person may stand up for his or her beliefs. Another person may follow rules without question.

Going against what usually is considered normal sometimes is called unethical behavior. However, what some people see as unethical may be considered ethical by others. Sometimes people become heroes because they risk their reputation for a belief that society may disapprove of.

ETHICAL FACE-OFF

See how your ethical views compare with those of your family and friends. Ask them these questions:

1. While shopping, you receive $10 in change. You should have received only $1. What would you do?

2. Is it okay to break a minor law such as by speeding or smoking if you know you won't get caught? Why or why not?

3. Laws about taxes, job applications, or insurance claims call for the absolute truth. Is it ever okay to lie in these situations if you do it to protect yourself or others? If so, when?

4. If you were the only witness to a murder, would you come forward to tell the police? What if you saw someone painting graffiti on a wall? Explain.

Points to Consider: EthicalMatters

How might your conscience influence your ethical behavior?

Give an example of how emotions can influence a person's behavior.

Are there people in your community or school who have had problems because of their ethical beliefs?

Chapter Overview

Issues that are highly emotional can help you define your ethics.

The stand you take in a complex ethical dilemma is based on your ethical code.

Having an ethical code and taking an ethical stand builds confidence in your ability to create a healthy situation for yourself and others.

Adults can be good examples of ethical behavior.

Ethical behavior is celebrated all over the world.

Ethics

CHAPTER 3

⬡

Under Fire

Ethics are different for everyone. They could be called **PersonalMatters.** Not everyone will agree with your ethics. Still, it's important to be aware of your ethical code and to follow it.

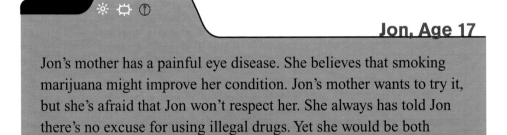

Jon, Age 17

Jon's mother has a painful eye disease. She believes that smoking marijuana might improve her condition. Jon's mother wants to try it, but she's afraid that Jon won't respect her. She always has told Jon there's no excuse for using illegal drugs. Yet she would be both buying and using illegal drugs. Jon wants to help his mother but isn't sure how.

Is Jon's mother wrong to want to try marijuana as a medicine? Is Jon wrong to want to help her? Do you think he should have less respect for his mother because she's not doing as she says?

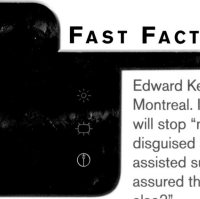

Edward Keyserlingk is a professor at McGill University in Montreal. In discussing legalized euthanasia, he wondered what will stop "nonvoluntary euthanasia, or even murder, from being disguised as assisted suicide. Since motives are so important in assisted suicide, as they are in euthanasia, is it possible to be assured that the motive was mercy as opposed to something else?"

Some topics or behaviors tend to generate strong emotions in people. Ethical issues often surface when the health, safety, or ability of people to choose are threatened. How are these issues related to ethics?

Euthanasia, or helping someone to kill himself or herself; euthanasia is sometimes called mercy killing.

Underage drinking

Child abuse, or mistreating a child

Capital punishment, or the death penalty

Hatred of people based on their ethnic background

Many teens have opinions about these issues. Your opinions may be different from other people's. Thinking about and discussing these issues helps you define your ethics.

Your Ethical Code

What is an ethical code? It's the entire system of beliefs that guide a person's ethical behavior. How do you decide your own code of ethics? Try the following self-assessment. It lists several characteristics that can help you decide what your ethical code is.

Finding Your Ethical Code

Read items 1–11 below. On another sheet of paper, write the number after each item that describes you best. Use this rating scale:

1 = Rarely   2 = Sometimes   3 = Most of the time

1. I can hold a belief even if others pressure me to give it up.	1	2	3
2. I am responsible and keep my word.	1	2	3
3. I am fair.	1	2	3
4. I am patient.	1	2	3
5. I am generous and kind.	1	2	3
6. I use logical ideas.	1	2	3
7. My life has order and predictability.	1	2	3
8. I am loyal and devoted to people and ideas.	1	2	3
9. I am courageous and determined about my beliefs.	1	2	3
10. I am humble and modest.	1	2	3
11. I use care before making decisions.	1	2	3

Add other characteristics that are important to you. Together, all these characteristics form the foundation of your code of ethics. Add up your points. The higher your point total, the more these characteristics are part of your ethical code.

The Importance of Having an Ethical Code

Why should you care about your code of ethics? It helps you to know what you believe or care stongly about when faced with challenges. It can help you define what it means to be a good person. It can help you decide the traits you respect in a friend or others. For example, your code of ethics may say that violence is unneeded. If so, you probably won't use violence.

A well-defined ethical code might help you make healthy choices. Ethical behavior can guide your decisions about using alcohol, tobacco, and other illegal drugs.

Adults Can Be Examples

Commonly, parents, teachers, and other adults are examples of acceptable behavior. This is behavior that most people approve of. Adults may tell you to stand up for what you believe or follow your dreams. Do adults have other guidelines for you? For example, do they tell you how to act at school or on a date? Are they clear about what happens if a rule is broken?

You can learn acceptable behavior by watching what most adults say and do. However, sometimes what they say doesn't match what they do. For example, your uncle may say that cigarette smoking is wrong and can cause serious health problems. Yet you know that he smokes. This may cause an ethical dilemma for you. You believe smoking is wrong, but the difference in your uncle's words and actions confuses you.

Celebrating Ethical Behavior

People worldwide celebrate the ethical behavior of people who came under fire. Many of these are adults that you might be interested in learning about. Some holidays also celebrate ethical action. Here are some examples of both:

January: Martin Luther King, Jr., was born. He fought against the separation of African Americans and whites. His fight was based on the belief that everyone has the right to equal treatment. He followed his belief and was killed because of it.

February: In some parts of the United States, President's Day is a holiday to honor great leaders including George Washington and Abraham Lincoln. Washington led an army of Americans against the British. Lincoln is remembered for his stand to free slaves, which led to the Civil War.

March: St. Patrick is the patron saint of Ireland. He is remembered for his bravery during his period of slavery in Ireland and peaceful return to the island.

April: Many people celebrate Arbor Day. It encourages people to preserve the environment by planting trees.

May: Buddhists remember Vesak day, a reminder of Buddha's birth, life of enlightenment, and death.

June: In Barcelona, Spain, St. John's Day is set aside for singing a love song to a loved one.

July: Each July 4 is set aside in the United States to celebrate freedom and independence.

August: Santa Rosa de Lima is celebrated in Peru. St. Rose spent a lifetime helping the sick, poor, and slaves.

September: Jewish New Year, Rosh Hashanah, occurs. A round loaf of challah bread is eaten. It is a reminder that life comes around again and allows for new beginnings.

October: Mohandas Gandhi was born in India. He lived a simple life and believed in nonviolence.

ETHICAL FACE-OFF

See how your ethical views compare with those of your family and friends. Ask them these questions:

1. If a coworker stole money from work, would you turn him or her in?

2. Is it acceptable to lie to someone if you think the truth would hurt the person?

3. You observe two people fighting. One is getting seriously injured. What would you do?

4. What would you do if you found the answer key to an upcoming test in one of your classes?

November: In the United States, a day each November is set aside as a reminder to be thankful.

December: In many places, the spirit of selflessness is remembered through the giving of gifts.

Points to Consider: PersonalMatters

What laws exist in your community that define ethical behavior?

From the self-assessment on page 25, choose three ethical characteristics that are most important to you. Why did you choose them?

What other events are celebrated around the world that illustrate ethical behavior or beliefs?

Chapter Overview

Many professions have a statement of ethics that people in the profession promise to follow. This statement is called professional ethics.

Friends are important for the social and emotional health of a teen. Dilemmas can occur between friends.

Sometimes ethical dilemmas result in new views of your relationships with others.

Ethics

CHAPTER 4

Standing Your Ground

FriendshipMatters might involve complicated situations with others that require you to consider your ethical code.

Professional Ethics

Many professional organizations have a statement of ethics that guide practitioners' behavior. For example, many doctors and nurses have the Hippocratic Oath. It describes ethical medical practices and behavior these professionals should follow. The oath states many ways that doctors should do no harm.

AT A GLANCE

In making ethical decisions, don't let rationalizations distract you. These ways to justify your decision are common, such as the following:

"Everybody's doing it."

"It isn't hurting anyone."

"I deserve it" or "I've got it coming."

"I was just doing it for that other person."

"The end justifies the means."

Psychiatrists, counselors, and other helping professionals also have a statement of ethics. For example, psychiatrists promise not to tell information that a patient gives them. Teachers and other educators have a code of ethics, too. It includes creating a safe learning environment and teaching appropriate academic skills.

Lawyers, architects, and religious leaders have ethical standards they follow. These standards often involve trust, honesty, and truthfulness. These standards of behavior are called professional ethics.

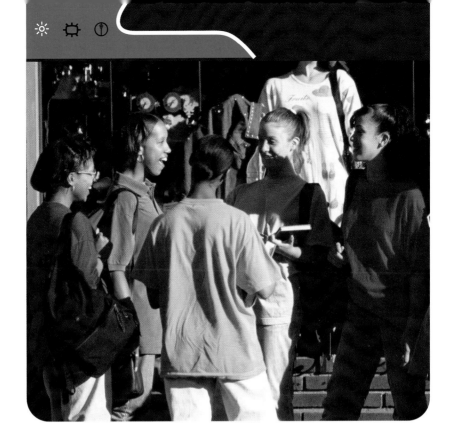

Cassandra, Age 15

Cassandra does everything with her friends. They hang out with each other at school. On weekends they hang out at each other's house.

Cassandra's friends recently bought her a ticket to a rock concert for her birthday. Cassandra's father doesn't know she has the ticket. He believes the musical group is evil, because their songs seem to encourage drug use, sexual behavior, and violence. The concert is Friday night, when Cassandra's father goes bowling. It's likely Cassandra could go without his knowing. What should Cassandra do?

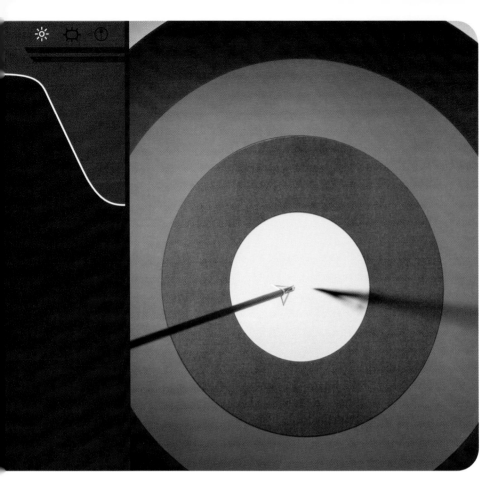

Your Circle of Friends

Nearly everyone has a circle of friends. Think of it as a target with four circles. You are at the center. Your view of the world is based on your experiences and character traits. You have a distinct personality, appearance, and code of ethics.

In the next circle are your best friends. You can share almost everything with them. Best friends can feel your feelings, finish your sentences, and laugh and cry with you. Sometimes you share so much that part of you seems to be missing when the friends are gone. Sometimes those friends can see things about you that you can't see. These friendships are usually healthy, fun, and satisfying. Such special friends probably share your code of ethics.

"My best friend has really changed. I don't know if I trust her anymore. She started smoking and pierced her tongue. She dresses in baggy clothes and sweat pants. Now she tells me she wants to shave her head. I'm just not into that stuff. I don't feel like we have anything in common anymore."
—Amanda, age 14

The third circle contains classmates and other friends. You may talk on the telephone and go to parties, movies, and other events together. Many of these people may have a code of ethics much like yours.

The fourth circle includes people with whom you share little. These people may be called acquaintances. They may attend school with you. You may be on a sports team together. You may discuss school-related things but rarely get together otherwise. You probably put little energy into sharing yourself with acquaintances. Their code of ethics may be like yours, or it may be very different.

Are your friendships founded on deep, shared experiences with a range of emotions? Do you have separate interests but share likes and dislikes? Can you laugh together? Can you disagree about things but compromise on important issues?

Ethical Dilemmas Between Friends

Friendship can be bittersweet. Having a best friend can be extremely satisfying. Likewise, losing a friend can feel like the end of the world. You may feel alone and sad for a long time.

Friendships improve social and emotional health. Sometimes teens may feel they would do anything to have or keep their friendships. But should they? This is where a code of ethics can guide behavior.

Maybe the people you hang around with have less respect for authority than you have. Maybe they've been caught shoplifting. Maybe they pressure you to try alcohol or other drugs. To fit into the group, you may feel you need "cool" clothes or the "right" hairstyle. It's possible to give away so much of yourself in a friendship that you lose your identity.

ETHICAL FACE-OFF

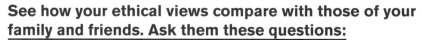

See how your ethical views compare with those of your family and friends. Ask them these questions:

1. What would you do if you accidentally broke something while shopping? Would the price of the item make a difference in the action you choose?

2. Your school grade point average (GPA) is 2.7 but falsely shows up on your records as 3.7. What would you do?

3. Would you let your friends have free food or products at the place you work?

4. What would you do if a classmate other than a friend was cheating in school?

It's not always easy to make friends. The more you admire someone, the more you want to please that person. The more you wish a group to accept you, the more you may avoid questioning their unhealthy behaviors. When friends go against your ethics, behaving ethically can be difficult.

Doing the right thing can be hard. But it's important to stick to your beliefs.

Points to Consider: FriendshipMatters

Why is it important for professions to have a code of ethics?

Do you think professional ethics are different from personal ethics? Do you see similarities between professional and personal ethics? Explain.

Using the target model described in this chapter, draw your circle of friends.

Describe an ethical dilemma that tests a friendship.

Chapter Overview

Communicating about ethical issues can be hard. The letters in TEENS DO TALK can help you remember some communication guidelines.

Your belief in yourself and your critical thinking skills are important in dealing with an ethical dilemma.

Using your ethical code to guide your thinking will help you find solutions to ethical dilemmas.

CHAPTER 5

✧

Communication and Critical Thinking

Critical thinking means that you will look deep into yourself to explore what you think and how you feel. Then you can use your skill and knowledge to solve ethical dilemmas. This critical thinking can be called **AnalyzingMatters.**

Teng, Age 16

Teng is a student in your class. His family recently moved here from another country. He wears the same clothes several days in a row. He brings his lunch from home. Usually he eats by himself at the "nerd table." No one ever sits by him or talks with him. You know he is the oldest of eight children. His parents, grandparents, brothers, and sisters live together in low-income housing. You decide to invite him to eat with you. Just then, three popular kids take his lunch and throw it in the garbage can.

Teng's situation presents an ethical dilemma. How would you respond in this situation? Here are a few options:

Confront the three popular students.

Be angry at the students but say nothing.

Pretend you never saw the incident.

Wait for a few minutes and then invite Teng to share your lunch with you.

Feel sorry for Teng.

Make yourself believe that Teng deserves the behavior.

Avoid thinking about Teng.

Tell your favorite teacher about the incident later in the day.

Immediately tell the lunchroom supervisor what you saw.

Dear Gabby: My best friend is captain of the gymnastics team, which I'm on, too. Whenever we have a meet, she always gets sick or hurts her knee. She hasn't competed in the last three meets. She told me in private that she's faking it! She likes being captain but is afraid people will find out she's not good enough. This bugs me. If she's captain, shouldn't she put herself out there along with the rest of us? I feel like telling our coach, but my friend would hate me if she found out. Any advice? Signed, Bugged

Dear Bugged: You have a right to be irritated. Being team captain is a big responsibility. Your team should be able to look to your friend for leadership. Lying about injuries is dishonest, not to mention disrespectful of the team. The right thing to do is talk to your friend first. Tell her that lying is dishonest and she's letting down the team. If she won't change her behavior, then tell the coach. Let your coach handle it from there. It takes courage to do what you're doing. Good luck!

Communicating About Ethical Issues

When you have a problem, you might want to communicate with someone you trust. In the situation involving Teng, the best course of action might be to find someone who will listen to you. If the person you choose to talk with is part of the dilemma, you may need courage to begin. It may be difficult, but openness and honesty are the best attitudes.

Even newborn babies can empathize with others. This has led some researchers to believe some aspects of empathy are instinctive. For example, infants often reach out and touch others who are in distress. In hospitals, one infant's crying often leads to a roomful of crying babies.

One guide to start communicating is to use the letters TEENS DO TALK. They can help you focus on a topic that is troubling you.

Talk about talking. Talking about problems can be hard. Be direct. Inform the other person that you face an ethical dilemma and want to talk about it. Admit that the topic or issue is difficult or even embarrassing to discuss. This may help the other person be sympathetic to you.

Encourage others. Encourage the other person to share his or her views. Seek the person's advice and comments. Remember, you may be the one needing encouragement.

Empathize. Let your words and actions show that you empathize, or understand the other person's feelings. Work hard to clearly understand the other person's situation, feelings, emotions, and reasons.

Nonverbal language is important. Along with your words, you send messages nonverbally. Your body positions, facial expressions, eye contact, and hand motions can express your real feelings. For example, looking at the ground or folding your arms may show anger or boredom. Leaning toward the speaker may show interest. Be aware of your body language and try to match it to your words.

Stick to the subject. Stay focused! Don't clutter your important ethical discussions with unimportant information and stories. Focus on the dilemma. If you want to talk about stealing, don't start discussing the latest CD you bought. Ask the other person to stick to the subject, too.

Discover the meaning. As you discuss the problem, look for the speaker's main message. You may need to ask for more information if you don't understand.

Open a conversation. Many discussions of ethics can be serious and difficult. Distractions can make serious discussions seem less meaningful. Choose an appropriate time to start a difficult conversation. Wait until the person can concentrate fully on your message.

Tone sends a message. Along with words and gestures, your tone sends messages. Tone includes the loudness or softness of your voice. Many ethical issues stir up intense emotions. Tone can either support or confuse your message. Try to match your tone to the message.

"Great spirits have always encountered violent opposition from mediocre minds."—Albert Einstein

Attention! Ethical issues require concentration. Make sure everyone is focused on what's being said and how. For example, don't look out the window as if you don't care. Watch and listen for feedback so you know you've understood others correctly. You want them to pay attention to you, too.

Let yourself and others finish sentences. Don't interrupt! Resist jumping into the conversation with a bunch of "yeah, buts" or "howevers." As you speak, don't keep listeners waiting too long before you finish your sentences.

Know what you want to say. Many ethical discussions are about areas such as medicine, law, science, or psychology that use special words. Use the appropriate language when discussing a specific issue. Check often to see that your listener understands your meaning.

Critical Thinking

Critical thinking skills are important for ethical discussions. Critical thinking means gathering, analyzing, and applying information about an issue before making a decision. What are your gut feelings and behaviors as you react to a situation? Do you have all the information you need? What resources can help you decide? Are you willing to compromise to resolve a dilemma?

It may be simple to decide where you stand in certain ethical situations. It may be easy if you don't know the other person and can walk away. Avoiding the situation, however, may make it worse.

You can respond to an ethical dilemma in many ways. You might avoid it. You might discuss it and try to arrive at a compromise.

Peter, Age 16

Peter knows several classmates who use dangerous and illegal muscle-building drugs. The students' strength has increased so much that they have set records and won trophies for the school. Teachers and coaches favor these students. The community is proud of them, and they have appeared in the local media. They're heroes to grade-school children.

Should Peter avoid the problem? Should he tell community and school members what he knows about the students' drug use? What would you do if you were Peter?

LouEllen, Age 17

LouEllen's best friend, Jeanne, is seriously dating a guy who LouEllen believes physically abuses Jeanne. Lately, Jeanne and LouEllen have become distant. LouEllen sees Jeanne less often. When they do get together, LouEllen notices that Jeanne has bruises in unusual places. Jeanne can't explain them easily.

Should LouEllen acknowledge or avoid the problem? Should she confront Jeanne and offer help? What would you do if you were LouEllen? Use your critical thinking skills to help decide the ethical thing to do.

ETHICAL FACE-OFF

See how your ethical views compare with those of your family and friends. Ask them these questions:

1. Is it okay to commit a serious crime if you know you won't get caught?

2. In a parking lot, your car door damages the new car parked next to you. What would you do?

3. What would you do if you borrowed $10 from someone and the person forgot?

4. What would you do if a good friend or family member committed a crime in which someone was hurt?

Points to Consider: Analyzing Matters

Why do you think ethical discussions stir up emotions?

Why is it important to empathize during an ethical discussion?

Give an example of how your body language can give clues to your ethical beliefs.

How have you responded to a recent ethical dilemma? What happened?

Chapter Overview

There are five steps you can follow to handle an ethical dilemma.

Ethical courage is the ability to be ethical in spite of pressure.

Schools are part of the community and often teach students ethical behavior.

Relationships with others in the community are an important part of your developing ethics.

The 10 Confirming Clues can help you judge if an action is ethical.

CHAPTER 6

⌂

Community Ethics

Ethical dilemmas present themselves everywhere you go. You know about issues with opposing points of view. Most of these dilemmas have no simple solution. Throughout history, ethical dilemmas have torn at the core of individuals, communities, families, and countries. Your ethics help mold your behavior to deal with dilemmas and could be called **CharacterMatters**.

FAST FACT

Socially responsible investing lets people support their communities, the environment, and other concerns. They do this through their investment of savings or retirement money. A social investor can choose to invest money only with companies involved in socially or environmentally responsible work.

Imagine this ethical issue. A local factory is suspected of illegally dumping chemicals into a lake and causing environmental pollution. Chemicals released into the air and water may be killing fish. A large number of people, including children, have reported skin and breathing problems. Most people in the community work in this factory.

Is this an ethical dilemma? What could you do? One path might be to speak out in defense of clean air and water. Follow these steps.

1. **Decide if there is an ethical dilemma.** What is the real concern, question, debate, or difference of opinion?

2. **Educate yourself.** Get the facts about the situation. Consider the reliability of your sources.

3. **Communicate your concern to others.** Enlist the help of people who can help you work on a solution to the problem. Who are the people who can influence the decision?

4. **Decide if there is something you can do to make a difference.** You might think about talking with a leader in the factory. You could ask city leaders to look into the issue. Make a list of ideas. Decide which options have the greatest benefits or cause the least harm. Discard obviously illegal or improper activities.

5. **Decide on a plan of action and follow through.** Think of a plan with the greatest benefit and fewest risks. Afterward, if you think the solution didn't work, go back to step 4. Be ready to consider new information that might change your decision.

Your ethics can provide you with the courage and ability to be true to yourself. Facing an ethical dilemma might mean you have new things to learn about yourself. Good decisions may require you to spend time alone with the knowledge and information you've gathered. Look at the following self-assessment. It can help you see how much courage you have to hold to your ethics when you know you're right.

My Ethical Courage

Read items 1–11 below. On separate paper, write the number following each item that describes you best. Use this rating scale:

1 = Rarely   2 = Sometimes   3 = Most of the time

	1	2	3
1. I question rules that seem unfair or wrong.	1	2	3
2. I'm honest.	1	2	3
3. I expect my friends to tell me the truth.	1	2	3
4. I trust adults.	1	2	3
5. I listen to my conscience.	1	2	3
6. I stand up for my friends.	1	2	3
7. I avoid lying.	1	2	3
8. I avoid exaggerating.	1	2	3
9. I treat others fairly.	1	2	3
10. I make healthy choices.	1	2	3
11. I make independent decisions.	1	2	3

The closer your total is to 33, the more ethical courage you probably have. For any items on which you have a 1 or 2, you might want to practice to improve them. It is possible to learn how to have ethical courage.

FAST FACT

A 1998 survey asked more than 20,000 middle and high school students about their ethical behavior. Nearly half of them said they stole. Seven in ten admitted to cheating on a test within the previous year. And 92 percent of the high school students said they had lied at least once in the past year. More than a third said they would lie to get a good job. Interestingly, about 97 percent of the students said, "It's important for me to be a person with good character."

Ethics in School

Some schools teach conflict resolution skills. The ability to solve conflicts fairly and without force is a skill that teens can learn and practice. These skills are part of building who you are ethically.

Some schools teach character skills. This may be called character development. One way schools help students develop ethical behavior is through group projects. Group members discuss their perspectives and common goals. They learn to work out their differences. They learn how to disagree with others respectfully. These are all valuable skills for making ethical decisions.

Some schools have created opportunities for service learning. Service learning can create a bridge between students and the community. For example, some students help deliver food to older people in the community. It's been said that commercial advertising teaches you what you don't have. But service teaches you what you do have. Service learning shows you ways that your work positively affects other people's lives.

Here are three other tests to decide if you're doing the right thing:

Golden rule: Are you treating someone else the way you would like to be treated? If not, you might want to rethink your behavior.

Parent on your shoulder: Would you be comfortable with your behavior if a parent or other respected adult were watching you? If you're uncomfortable with that thought, your behavior may not be ethical.

Publicity: How would you feel if your reasoning or actions were published in tomorrow's news reports? If you'd be embarrassed, you probably should be doing something else.

Work in Progress

To develop ethical characteristics is to have a work in progress. Your relationships with others have a powerful influence on character development. Virtuous, or positive, ethical behaviors, provide a standard. Ethics may not change, but they may get challenged. Following your conscience and regulating your behavior according to the situation will be part of the defining work you do. Some helpful relationships are those between adult-young person or parent-child.

Acting on your ethics shows that you are self-confident and believe in your ability to figure things out. It shows that you respect yourself and others.

People who behave ethically want to understand the world around them. They can reason and use logical thought. They think for themselves.

Each ethical challenge results in more questions and more decisions. What matters most to you? There is no right answer for every person. The same solution does not fit all people. There is no bar code on your forehead for scanning the possibilities.

Ethical Actions: The Final Step

This book has been about making decisions that support your beliefs and values. You have read what ethics are and why they're important. You've had an opportunity to practice identifying, developing, and using your personal code of ethics. Now it's time to put all you know about ethics into action.

Did I Do The Right Thing?

You will face many ethical dilemmas in the future. Here are 10 Confirming Clues to help you feel confident that you have done the right thing! Think of a situation you've been in or face now. Then for each question below, write yes or no on a separate sheet of paper.

My ethical action:

1. was safe . . . . **Yes**   **No**

2. was legal . . . . **Yes**   **No**

3. felt good . . . . **Yes**   **No**

4. felt right . . . . **Yes**   **No**

5. showed respect for myself and others . . . . **Yes**   **No**

6. was healthy . . . . **Yes**   **No**

7. demonstrated good character . . . . **Yes**   **No**

8. was helpful . . . . **Yes**   **No**

9. was based on knowledge . . . . **Yes**   **No**

10. would be my choice again . . . . **Yes**   **No**

The more times you answered yes, the more you can be sure your choice probably was the right one. It means that you're probably happy with your action. You will be able to sleep with a clear conscience. When you know you're right, do it! Enjoy the ride!

ETHICAL FACE-OFF

See how your ethical views compare with those of your family and friends. Ask them these questions:

1. Is it okay to take little things such as office supplies from your work?

2. What would you do if you knew a valuable item was incorrectly priced and the sales clerk didn't notice it? For example, a $500 baseball card was priced at $50.

3. What would you do if you were driving or riding in a car and you saw someone lying by the road?

Points to Consider: CharacterMatters

How is self-confidence developed when you take an ethical stand?

How is ethical behavior demonstrated in your neighborhood and community?

Consider a recent health-related decision that you made. Use the 10 Confirming Clues to help you decide if it was ethical.

NOTE

At publication, all resources listed here were accurate and appropriate to the topics covered in this book. Addresses and phone numbers may change. When visiting Internet sites and links, use good judgment.

Useful Addresses

Josephson Institute of Ethics
4640 Admiralty Way, Suite 1001
Marina del Rey, CA 90292-6610
www.charactercounts.org

Corporation for National Service
1201 New York Avenue Northwest
Washington, DC 20525
www.nationalservice.org

National Youth Leadership Council
1910 West County Road B
Roseville, MN 55113
www.nylc.org

Internet Sites

Cyberangels
www.cyberangels.org
Safety and fun for kids on the Internet

KidsHealth for Teens
www.kidshealth.org/teen
Games and information devoted to the health of teens

For More Information

For Further Reading

Columbia University's Health Education Program. *The Go Ask Alice Book of Answers: A Guide to Good Physical, Sexual, and Emotional Health.* New York: Holt, 1999.

Covey, Sean. *The Seven Habits of Highly Effective Teens.* New York: Simon and Schuster, 1998.

Kimball, Gayle. *The Teen Trip: The Complete Resource Guide.* Chico, CA: Equality Press, 1997.

Wandberg, Robert. *Conflict Resolution: Communication, Cooperation, Compromise.* Mankato, MN: Capstone, 2001.

Wandberg, Robert. *Making Tough Decisions: Working Through Hard Choices.* Mankato, MN: Capstone, 2001.

Glossary

acceptable behavior (ak-SEP-tuh-buhl bi-HAYV-yur)—actions that most people approve of; acceptable behavior usually is based on doing the right thing.

community health (kuh-MYOO-nuh-tee HELTH)—the social, environmental, physical, and emotional well-being of a neighborhood and group of people

empathize (EM-puh-thize)—to understand someone's feelings

ethic (ETH-ik)—a standard of right and wrong that guides a person's thinking and behavior

ethical code (ETH-uh-kuhl KODE)—an entire system of beliefs that guide a person's ethical behavior

ethical dilemma (ETH-uh-kuhl duh-LEM-uh)—a problem that may have no clear right or wrong answers

moral behavior (MOH-ruhl bi-HAYV-yur)—behavior that follows a standard of right and wrong

standard (STAN-durd)—normal, regular, customary

universal ethics (yoo-nuh-VER-suhl ETH-iks)—a set of ethics that societies throughout the world seem to agree on; universal ethics include respect, responsibility, fairness, caring, citizenship, and trustworthiness.

virtuous (VUR-choo-uhss)—honest and respectable ethical behavior

Index

actions. *See* ethics
adults, 26–27, 54, 56
alcohol, 11, 17, 26, 37
AnalyzingMatters, 41
assisted suicide. *See* euthanasia

behavior, 8, 11, 15, 17, 18, 19, 24, 31,
     46, 51, 56
   acceptible, 5, 8, 10, 12, 26, 27
   ethical, 5, 12, 17, 18, 20, 24, 27, 38,
     55, 56, 57, 59
   unethical, 6, 20
beliefs, 7, 8, 10, 11, 12, 17, 19, 20, 24,
     25, 26, 38, 57
boundaries, 15
Buddha, 28

challenge, 26, 57
character, 55, 58
CharacterMatters, 51
cheating, 18, 29, 38, 55
choices, 5, 6, 7, 8, 17, 18, 24, 26, 58
cigarettes, 9, 26. *See also* smoking;
     tobacco
communication, 43–46, 52
community, 47, 51–52, 55. *See also*
     health
ComplexMatters, 6
compromise, 36, 46
confidentiality, 9, 32
conflicts, 15, 55
confrontation, 42, 48
conscience, 15, 16, 56, 58
courage, 25, 43, 53, 54
critical thinking, 41, 46–48

death or dying, 8, 9, 19, 20, 24, 27
death penalty, 11, 24
decisions, 5, 16, 18, 25, 32, 46, 53, 54,
     55, 56, 57

dilemmas. *See* ethics
doctors, 9, 31
drinking, 7, 24
drugs, 9, 10, 23, 26, 33, 37. *See also*
     marijuana

empathy, 44
environment, 52
ethics
   actions, 5, 6, 8, 17, 20, 27, 53, 56,
     57, 58
   code, 23, 24–26, 31, 34, 35, 37, 57
   defining, 5, 24
   dilemmas, 6, 12, 20, 41, 42, 43, 44,
     45, 46, 47, 51, 52, 53
   discussions, 44–46
   and friends, 34–38, 43
   professional, 31–32
   right, 5, 6, 8, 12, 15, 17, 19, 20, 38,
     53, 58
   standards, 5, 19, 32, 56
   universal, 18, 19
   views, 21, 29, 38, 49, 59
   wrong, 5, 8, 10, 15, 19, 20
EthicalMatters, 15
euthanasia, 24

fairness, 18, 25, 54, 55
family, 10, 16, 18, 20, 29, 38, 49, 51
feelings, 12, 34, 41, 44, 46
friends, 6, 16, 17, 18, 26, 29, 33,
     34–38, 43, 49, 54, 59
FriendshipMatters, 31

Gandhi, Mohandas, 19, 28

health, 17, 24, 26, 34, 54
   community, 12
   emotional, 37
   family, 12, 23